D0903256

Manuela Sanne · Ariane Rudolph · Catherine Lauer-Walker

Tuffi – an Elephantastic Story

Idea Simone Jacken

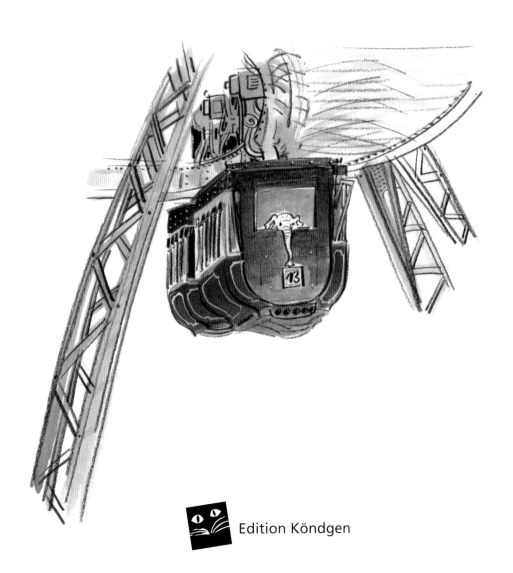

Edition Köndgen

Do you know India so far away
where elephants live for fun?
Tuffi lived there, as bright as day
with uncles and aunts and also her mum.

Tuffi with her flappy ears,
the maharaja's palace her home,
the royal favourite sweet and dear,
love and luxury and never a moan.

Mahout the pretty, little elephant boy,
wondered how clever she could be,
always cheerful and full of joy,
such a purely, magnificent girl was she.

For this little girl so sweet
The dealer paid really a lot,
„She'll be loved by all she meets
In the circus she'll be really the top."

„Oops", she thought, „a circus is fine.
I'll be a famous star, my dear!
In the ring I'll have a wonderful time."
And then she was hitched to a lot of gear.

Around her tummy a rope was bound
and fixed to a crank both firm and safe.
She sailed to the deck to a lovely place
and there she was cheerfully unwound.

On cushions made of velvet and silk,
sat a hamper for Tuffi so neat.
Filled to the brim with goodies and milk,
„This," she thought, „was just the treat."

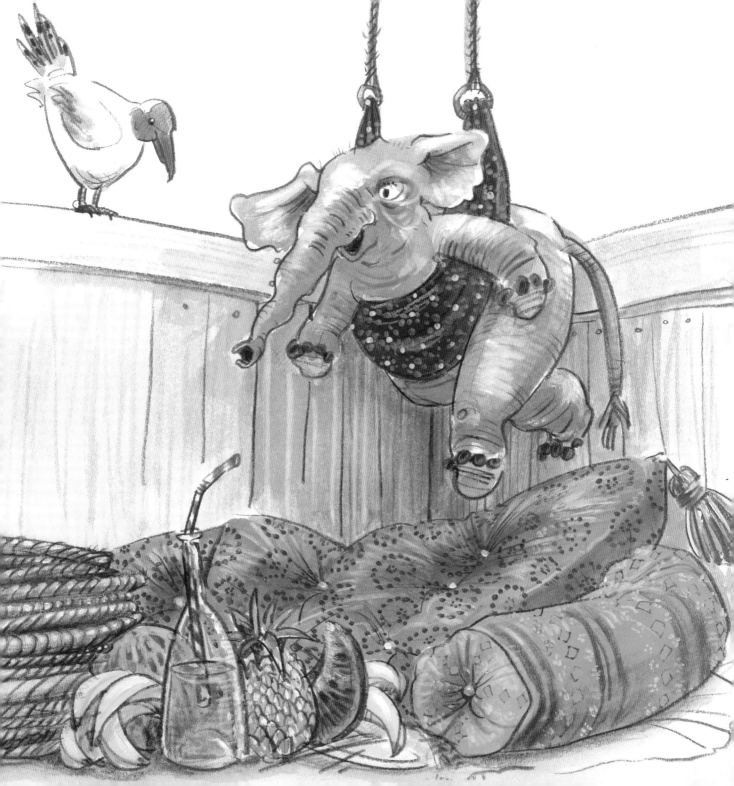

Then, suddenly, she felt big hot tears.
Saying farewell was always hard.
And then a trip so full of fears,
on a huge, big ship without her guard.

On the quay her family side by side,
the prince, Mahout and Robin the hare.
„Tuffi, forget us not!" they cried,
„Bon voyage! Adieu and take care!"

They sailed to Genoa so grand
and onto a big silver bird she was led.
They flew to some far-off land,
but Tuffi's heart was feeling dread.

Under her feet the firm land,
at last she reached old Germany.
The circus director gave her his hand
and Tuffi's heart was full of harmony.

Such a sweet man, director Franz,
„Come, meet my children my dear."
Son Harry asked her for a dance,
daughter Franzi tickled her ear.

In the circus she had a wonderful time,
she was quickly friends with all to see.
But one little thing just wasn't so fine,
it really was not her cup of tea.

Instead of her room in the palace so fair,
she was stuffed in a stall so small.
The pushing and shoving was hardly to bear,
Nights she hated it most of all.

Every morning after the wake-up call,
she and Harry walked through the town.
Tuffi could find such wonderful stalls
and she nibbled and nibbled till she was full and round.

They had great fun and many a caper,
and in Oberhausen with real know-how,
a bunch of flowers she handed the mayor
with swaying hips and a pretty bow.

Up the scaffold she smartly climbed,
then off to the harbour in Duisburg so old.
Soon she was surrounded so kind,
with reporters and photographers bold.

For the circus it was wonderful publicity.
Director Sand had the following plan.
„Tuffi", he told her explicitly,
„In Wuppertal you'll ride in the Schwebebahn!"

Directly he picked up the phone,
and this was how it was done,
Wuppertal was their next home,
so off they went at the shot of a gun.

But something weighed on her little heart.
Early this morning was the big ride.
Much better to train and eat apple tart
and practise for the first performance of her life.

„Not to worry, sweetie-pie,“
said father and son together as one.
„You'll ride in a train in the blue, blue sky.
Come along Franzi, give Tuffi a bun.“

Off they went at an easy trot
to the station in Barmen so fine.
There were lots of tickets to be bought.
Behind them the press in a long, long line.

The man in the office wondered; „What's this? What's this?
She's much too heavy, oh dear, oh dear!“
Franz clapped her head and gave her a kiss.
„We'll buy 10 tickets, is that now clear?“

The press were all pushing like wild,
and making snapshots like mad.
„Eh!“ shouted Harry, „She's just a child.
Stop the pushing. Keep back! Keep back!“

Harry pulled and Franzi pushed her,
„I want to go home. I want my mum.
This is awful, I need a breather,
I want to see Mahmout and have some fun."

Tuffi felt sick and wanted the ground.
Stuffed in here was worse than the cage.
Loud voices and laughing all around.
Tuffi was slowly getting into a rage.

„I'm stuck here," she thought with fear,
„Maybe I can get through the floor."
Trumpeting loud, „I'm getting out of here."
She charged at what she thought was the door.

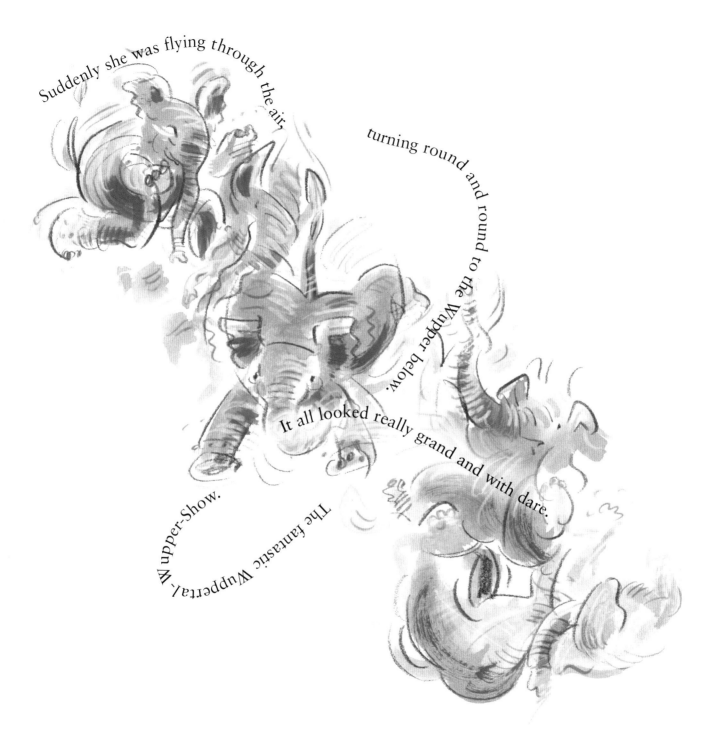

Suddenly she was flying through the air, turning round and round to the Wupper below. It all looked really grand and with dare. The fantastic Wuppertal-Wupper-Show.

At the next station they came to a stop.
The trip ended here for all and one.
Harry who was running on the spot,
set off quickly at a very fast run.

There she stood in the water knee-deep,
a couple of scratches here and there.
A little bit pale around her cheeks
and a few little scrapes on her botty so bare.

Harry hugged his darling beau,
stuck some plasters on her side.
Loudly he promised, „After this great show,
you're our biggest star. WOW! What a ride!"

Up the hill together they whirled,
everyone clapping and jumping for joy.
Here comes Tuffi the marvellous girl
and at her side the sweet circus boy.

Oh, my goodness, look at the crowd.
Tuffi was their princess so sweet.
They were all terrifically proud,
to give her Highness a wonderful treat.

The circus was filled up to the brim,
director Franz announced with glee.
„Ladies and gentlemen", he said with a grin,
„The star of the show, the daring Tufee."

And, oh my goodness, what a show they gave.
Everyone whistled and clapped with delight.
All the elephants so cheerful and brave
and last but not least our Tuffi so bright.

The press were being very teased.
Where was the photo of our beautiful doll?
The famous Tuffi was very pleased,
so cute, so sweet and loved by all.

Not one photo to be had.
Tuffi was too clever, too quick.
The press thought this was really bad.
But everyone loved her beautiful trick.

Tuffi sniggered out quite loud,
„Now its time to have a rest."
She dreamed of lying on a cloud
with satin sheets of only the best.

And from India so far away,
where elephants jump and run.
Came Tuffi here as bright as day.
Full of mischief and full of fun.

Her life was long and full of beauty.
Loved by all she did her duty.
We in Wuppertal all know her story.
She will live on in all her glory.

What really happened ...

Tuffi was born in freedom in 1946. In those days it was standard procedure to catch wild elephants, tame them and use them later as working animals. But Tuffi was much too young and was not allowed to carry any heavy loads, to lift or pull anything of any weight. Because it always cost so much to feed a baby elephant till it was strong enough, Tuffi was sold to the circus Franz Althoff in Germany. She spent her trip on the ship in a small transport box which she probably did not enjoy very much. There was one thing she did learn though; the way out was where the light came in.

She quickly settled into circus life. As the smallest elephant girl, not only eager to learn but also with a lovely, cheerful character, she proved to be the ideal advertising character for the travelling circus. She never lost her temper, neither during a tram journey in a number of towns nor during a harbour tour in Duisburg. She transported a crate of beer to the scaffolding in Solingen, emptied a holy-water well together with the other circus elephants in Altötting and presented the Town Mayor of Oberhausen with a bunch of flowers.

In 1950 Circus Althoff arrived in Wuppertal. Although the authorities were not over keen on Tuffi's trip on the suspension railway and were reluctant to permit it, it eventually did take place. The streets were lined with crowds when on Friday, 21 July 1950, Tuffi and her companions set off. These included the circus director, his twelve-year-old son Harry and, of course, his two-year-old daughter Franziska as well.

At the suspension railway station Alter Markt, at exactly 10.30, the director bought tickets for the second class carriage and together with members of the press they all got into carriage number 13. Contrary to all the agreements made beforehand, more and more photographers and reporters elbowed their way into the overcrowded compartment.

Harry Althoff explained later that everything had been too much for Tuffi. The cramped compartment, all the noise and shouting, the squealing of the carriage wheels and the swaying of the suspension railway, but above all it was the commotion and movement behind Tuffi's back, (elephants can't look behind them) which agitated her and triggered off her panic attack.

No stop sign could hold Tuffi back; she saw the light and using all her weight she just broke through the window of the carriage. After less that two minutes journey she went flying down to the Wupper ten metres below her. Fortunately she landed quite softly in a muddy part of the river and apart from a few scratches here or there she was almost unharmed.

Because of all the turmoil during the suspension railway journey, not one photograph was made of Tuffi's „flight". The postcard of the leap which was later issued was only a photomontage.

Circus director Franz Althoff and the head of the Wuppertal Transport Services were sentenced to fines for not only „endangering traffic but also causing bodily harm through negligence".

Tuffi performed for 18 years in Circus Althoff. She continued to travel on the train and the tram but she never ever got in a suspension railway again, even though she visited Wuppertal several times. In 1968 the Franz Althoff circus was dissolved and several of the elephants, including Tuffi, went to the French circus Alexis Gruss. Tuffi lived and worked there till her death in 1989. She died at the age of 43 in their winter quarters.

Directly opposite the house where Friedrich Engels was born, even today you can see the place where Tuffi jumped into the Wupper.

Manuela Sanne was born in 1962 in Paderborn, Germany and has worked as a bookseller in Wuppertal since 1983. She is particularly interested in literature for children and young adults. She has long been fascinated by verse and rhyme as a special form of expression. On a number of occasions she has successfully participated in writing competitions with her humorous poems.

Ariane Rudolph was born in 1966 in Düsseldorf and is a graduate designer with the main focus on illustration. She is a freelance graphic designer and illustrator and lives with her family in Wuppertal.

Simone Jacken, who lives with her family in Wuppertal, was born in 1960. As a pedagogue she promotes and encourages reading in schools and libraries and carries out book presentations in nurseries and parishes. She is a passionate fan of Astrid Lindgren and Cornelia Funke.

Catherine Lauer-Walker, English trainer and translator, was born in Scotland, but has lived in Wuppertal for many years. In her English school in Wuppertal she teaches English to adults and also in companies. She loves literature and writes poems and prose. She is also the creator and producer of a Learn CD – *Tailor-made for you – Love your tenses.*

More about Tuffi:
www.tuffiwuppertal.de

The Edition Köndgen publishes books and sells gift articles to do with Wuppertal, Schwelm and the Bergisches Land. The manifold facets of this region are presented in a lively and attractive way.

Bibliographical information of the German Library: the German Library records these publications in the German National Bibliography; detailed data can be found under *www.dnb.de.*

© All rights are reserved by Manuela Sanne, Ariane Rudolph and the publisher, the Edition Köndgen of Heinrich Köndgen GmbH. This work including all parts is protected by copyright. Any unauthorised broadcasting, public performance, copying or re-recording will constitute an infringement of copyright.

First published in German in Wuppertal in 2010
English Edition 2012
Design: Ariane Rudolph, Wuppertal
Translation: Catherine Lauer-Walker
Composition: Sandra Balcke, Wuppertal
Production: Banholzer Mediengestaltung, Rottweil
Printed and bound in Germany by Kessler Druck & Medien, Bobingen

ISBN 978-3-939843-29-0
www.edition.koendgen.de